TOM GATES

FIVE STAR STORIES

By Liz Pichon

Hidden in the book are

these FIVE funny star bugs

for you to FIND.

Answers on p.227. Don't cheat!

Excellent useful stone doodle

A MASSIVE thank-you to all these super-skilled folk for helping to make this Tom Gates book and for getting the books out into the world. You are all AMAZING!

My publisher Scholastic and all the lovely people there. Lauren, Catherine, Sarah, Jason, Andrew, Penelope, Claire, Toni, and the Scholastic Warwick Team!

My sister Lyn. Mark (as ever!).

Thanks to all the librarians, booksellers teachers, parents and anyone who has read or recommended a Tom Gates book.

Much love,
Liz xxxx

Derek starts with...

Did you see **THAT, TOM?**

WHAT? I say EXCITEDLY.

LOOK UP THERE!

Derek points to the skies.

WOW! I say and pull a face like I've just seen the most BRILLIANT thing **EVER.**

Marcus hears us and wants to know what's going on.

What are you two STARING at?

We've just seen something AMAZING!

Derek replies in a very convincing way.

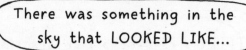

There was something in the sky that LOOKED LIKE...

(Another long pause.)

A **GLOWING** spaceship

WHEREABOUTS?

Marcus is looking **UP** and keeps checking the sky.

Ross White comes along with Trevor Peters and **N**orman. Two younger kids are behind them.

Hey! What's everyone looking at?

Trevor asks.

We SAW something hovering in the sky,

Derek explains.

Norman takes off his glasses and wipes the lenses on his arm, then puts them back on.

NOPE, still can't see anything.

It was probably an aeroplane, one little kid suggests sensibly.

It COULD have been...

BUT it was shaped like this - like an ACTUAL spaceship.

Derek uses his fingers to draw the shape of the spaceship in front of him.

Then he **GASPS** and says,

LOOK!
THERE IT IS AGAIN,
SEE!

"YES, I SAW IT TOO!"

I join in.

(Derek is SO good at this game.)

"What ARE **YOU TWO** looking AT? I can only see clouds."

Marcus thinks he's missed the 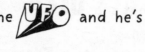 and he's annoyed about it.

The bell goes for the start of school. **Ding Ding Ding**

**AMY**, Florence and Indrani want to get past, but we're blocking the way.

"Move, please," **AMY** says, but everyone's looking up and no one budges.

"Hey, **AMY**, we just saw a real . That's an UNIDENTIFIED FLYING OBJECT!

We're waiting to see if it comes back," Marcus explains.

AMY doesn't look up, but Florence does...

... and so does Indrani.

"It could have been a **UFCP**," Indrani says.

"What's a **UFCP**?" I ask.

"**U**nidentified **F**lying **C**risp **P**acket.
When it's ∽♪ *windy* and some rubbish flies out of
the bin and ,,,ᵘᴾ into the air. Come on, let's go.
There's nothing there.

See you in class."
Indrani LAUGHS.

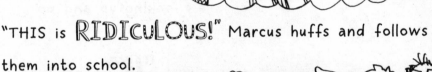

"THIS is RIDICULOUS!" Marcus huffs and follows
them into school.

Derek raises his eyebrows and whispers, "Eight, not bad!"
"Good thinking on the UFO, though my record still
stands at twelve kids <u>AND</u> Mr Sprocket looking
down a drain at nothing," I remind him.

"I might have to pretend there's a  again," Derek tells me. "It was GENIUS!

See you at break time."

As he heads off to Mr Sprocket's class, I call out,

"HEY, Derek - whatever you do, don't turn around."

(He turns around.)

"Ha! Got you..." I LAUGH.

"Every time... Nice one, Tom."

Mr Fullerman is at the back of the class, handing out today's worksheet. I sit down next to AMY and Marcus.

Straight away,

Marcus says,

"You didn't REALLY see a UFO, did you?"

(He's still cross with me.)

"Yes, we did, or we *thought* we did."

"You just like playing silly games," Marcus grumbles.

For a change, AMY agrees with Marcus.

"He's got a point, Tom."

"What do you mean?" I try and sound SURPRISED.

"You and Derek play a game where you look at NOTHING and see how many kids copy you," AMY calls me out.

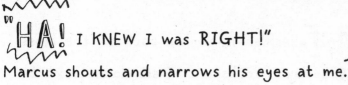 

"**HA!** I KNEW I was RIGHT!"

Marcus shouts and narrows his eyes at me.

"Sometimes we really DO see things!"

I say, but I'm not sure anyone believes me.

Then **AMY** nudges me.

"**HEY** – what's Caretaker Stan doing in the

school grounds? Is he ... dancing?" she asks us.

Marcus and I turn to look out of the window ...

... at nothing.

"You're right - this game is FUN!"
AMY LAUGHs to herself.

"I didn't look. I was watching Tom,"

Marcus mutters.

(He did look.) ☹

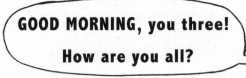

GOOD MORNING, you three! How are you all?

Mr Fullerman says cheerily and hands us a worksheet each.

For some reason, Marcus decides to tell him all about the game we've been playing.

"Sir, sir, Tom and **AMY** have been making up stories, sir. They keep getting me to look at things that aren't really there."

"EXCELLENT! Just what I want to hear. Today is all about making up stories."

Marcus is pulling faces like he doesn't understand.

"Sir?"

"You're **ALL** going to be writing FUNNY stories!"

Mr Fullerman explains.

"What kind of funny stories, sir?"

"Ones that make you LAUGH, Marcus!"

Then AMY reads the worksheet out.

"Listen up, both of you..."

OAKFIELD SCHOOL'S FIVE-STAR
* * * * *
FUNNY STORIES
We want you to write a
FUNNY STORY
for Oakfield School's first
EVER story book.
Write about anything that
makes YOU laugh, and if
your teacher gives you
* * * * * FIVE STARS,
your story will be
included in the book.

Here are some TIPS to get you started:

- Write about something that's made you laugh or that you find fun.
- Don't make your story too long.
- Read it out loud when you finish writing it.
- You could also write a funny poem too.
- Now – what are you waiting for? Get writing and MAKE US LAUGH!

* * * * *

This sounds FUN!

Marcus looks like he's plotting what to write about already.

"My story will be SO FUNNY! Do you want to know what it's about?" he asks.

(Not really.)

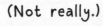

I'll start like this: once upon a time, there were some RIDICULOUS, ANNOYING kids who pretended to see UFOs. But really, they were just BUFFOONS who liked making things up.

 "Isn't a BUFFOON an animal?" I ask. Marcus stops talking for a second.

"Errrr, no."

"You've got loads of <u>other</u> FUNNY stories to tell, Marcus. Don't write about US," I say. "It's the ONLY FUNNY story I can think of right now," he says.

"Really? I can think of LOADS."

Then I remind him of a few.

16

"What about the time we went on the bug-collecting school trip and you fell in the mud? That was FUNNY!"

"Oh, yes, that WAS FUNNY!" AMY agrees.

"And remember when you both got stuck on the boating lake and the birds came and ate your sandwiches, Marcus?"

Ha! Ha!

"It wasn't that funny," Marcus grumbles.

(It really was.)

"How about when we thought you had a HUGE dog, but Tiny turned out to be ... tiny."

AMY and I are giggling a bit too loudly and
Mr Fullerman GLARES in our direction.
"I HOPE you're laughing at the story you're
about to write?"

He
he!

beady
eyes

"Sort of, sir..." I say quickly.

Marcus puts his hand up again to tell **Mr Fullerman**
something else.

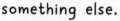

Sir!

Sir!

Sir!

"Yes, Marcus?"

"Errrr ... I've forgotten,"
Marcus says,

so **Mr Fullerman** moves on and CLAPS
his hands to get everyone's attention.

brain
strain

Marcus is still
trying to remember
what he wanted to say.

CLAP   CLAP

"Norman, glasses ON your face, please.
Amber, take the pencil OUT of your
mouth. Brad, don't do that. Brad!
Right, Class 5F, at today's assembly, we're all
in for a **TREAT!**"

When I hear the word TREAT, I think he's
talking about something to eat and I get excited.

I hear myself saying **OUT LOUD**,
"I LOVE TREATS!" (I'm not the only one.)
Brad shouts from the back of the class,

BISCUITS!

Everyone CHEERS at the idea of getting biscuits in
assembly.

Hooray!

"No, not biscuits, Brad, something even BETTER."

(What's better than biscuits?)

"Mrs Nap has a brand-new song to teach us
that includes a bit of..."

CAKE! Brad tries again.

"Not cake, Brad. WHISTLING," Mr Fullerman says.
"AND the recycled instrument orchestra will be
joining in," he adds like that's a good thing.

Everyone in the class starts to *whistle* to show
Mr Fullerman they can do it.

(Apart from me. I don't know why but
I can't *whistle*.)

whistle whistle
whistle
whistle whistle whistle

(me not
whistling)

"**Excellent whistling. Now let's see
if you can all stand up and push
your chairs in...**"

SCRAPE SCRAPE SCRAPE SCRAPE SCRAPE SCRAPE SCRAPE SCRAPE SCRAPE

"**QUIETLY...**"

Mr Fullerman says, but it's hard to hear over the
noise of the chairs and *whistling*.

There's (still) a LOT of tuneless *whistling* going on
as we walk to assembly. Marcus is doing it right
next to my EAR.

"I love *whistling*. It's so easy.
See. *Whistle*."

He keeps doing it...

whistle whistle
PEEP
whistle

I try and ignore him when I notice there's a
BIG BLOB of chewing gum on the floor.

Using my EXPERT swerving skills, I avoid
the gum and I warn Marcus
because I am a good person.

"Hey, Marcus. Look out for the—"

"Nice try, Tom. I'm not falling for that
TRICK again," he says ...

... and steps right in the gum.
"WHO PUT THAT THERE?"

Was it you, Tom?

Marcus tries to BLAME me for the gum. Now every time he takes a step it gets STUCK. At least he's stopped *whistling* now.

SIR, I've got chewing gum on the bottom of my shoe.

Mr Fullerman hands him a tissue.

For goodness' sake, Marcus, hurry up. Mrs Nap is waiting for us to sit down.

Marcus has to hop the rest of the way, then sits down dramatically like his foot's been injured. He grumbles as he tries to get the gum off.

This is ridiculous.

"I did try and tell you. You didn't listen to me," I enjoy reminding him.

Mrs Nap is looking especially HAPPY today, chatting to the recycled instrument orchestra kids who are ready to play their "guitars". They look like they're made from cardboard boxes, elastic bands and sticky tape. (LOTS of sticky tape.)

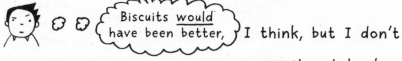

Biscuits would have been better, I think, but I don't say it out loud.

"Good morning. Is everyone OK?"
Mrs Nap asks us.
"Yes, Mrs Nap," we all say.

Marcus is still grumbling about his sticky gum foot.

GRUMBLE

 "Today I'll be teaching you my
BRAND-NEW SONG!"

she says excitedly.

"Can you all whistle?" she asks, which makes the

whole school start *whistling* very tunelessly.

Peep PEEP whistle whistle peep peep whistle

Everyone joins in ... apart from <u>me.</u> I keep trying

but nothing that sounds like a *whistle* is coming out.

 **M**rs **N**ap *whistles* the simple tune for

us to copy.

whistle *whistle* whistle whistle whistle

She repeats it a few times, but I've given up.

rrrasssp

"Anyone who can't whistle, clap your hands instead!" she says, looking straight at me.

"After **FOUR**, everyone.

One, two..."

CLAP
CLAP CLAP

The recycled orchestra starts too **EARLY** and there are already a few elastic bands

pinging and twanging...

Twang Twang Twang Ping Twang

(They don't sound much like guitars, either.)

I'm doing my best not to LAUGH as I don't want

to get into trouble with Mr Fullerman or get the

STARE OF DOOM.

Looking around at the other teachers in the hall, I

can see I'm not the only one trying not to LAUGH.

shaking shoulders

Meanwhile ... Mrs Nap is trying her very best to

teach us the NEW SONG.

(This is going to be a very long assembly...)

"Don't feel gloomy
Don't feel sad,
There's so much fun
to be had!
Forget all the things
That make you bristle,
Sing along with me,
It's time to WHISTLE."

Peep... Peep... Peep... Peep... Peep...
Peep... Peep... Peep...
Peep... Peep... Peep...

whistle whistle whistle

Mrs Nap sings the song over and over and over
again. She wants the song to get stuck in our heads
so we remember it. (It's working.)

Everyone around me is having no problem at all *whistling* away.

nothing

Marcus is *whistling* AND looking smug at the same time. I do a pretend *whistle* without making a sound to blend in, which sort of works.

Mrs Nap does her best to try and keep us all on track, but it's a bit ... difficult.

She's doing a lot of POINTING ☞ and encouraging FACIAL EXPRESSIONS at the recycled orchestra as they carry on PINGING. Finally, Mrs Nap brings us to a STOP with her hands and one more elastic band pings from one of the "guitars".

"That was TERRIBLE,"
AMY says and pulls a face at me.

"It was sort of FUNNY, though, wasn't it?"
I point out.

Then Marcus suddenly *LEANS* in and adds,

"You can't whistle, can you, Tom?"

"Eeeerrrr, yes I can."

"Go on then?"

Before Marcus forces me to *whistle,*

another PINGING

elastic band flies through the air and 3

Mrs Worthington CATCHES it with one hand!

(Mrs Worthington being impressive.)

We all `CHEER!`

It's the best thing about assembly.

(So far.)

Mrs Worthington takes a BOW, then holds up the same book Mr Fullerman showed us.

"Right, Oakfield School, do you all know what this is?" she asks.

IT'S A BOOK!

someone (Brad Galloway) shouts from the back of the hall.

"Yes, but what kind of book is it?"

A small BOOK!

Mrs Worthington ignores Brad and begins to explain about the school story book and how we should all have a go at writing something FUNNY.

A little kid right at the front puts up their hand.

Can I write a story about chocolate, Mrs Worthington?

"Yes, of course, Dawn. Who wouldn't want to read a story about chocolate?"

ME! I don't like chocolate, some other kid shouts from the back.

(I GASP. Who knew that was even possible?)

Then Norman puts up his hand.

"Can I write about Dragons and cheese, Mrs Worthington?"

"That sounds exciting, Norman, but not all the stories have to include food," she replies.

Now Mrs Worthington's said "FOOD",
that's the only thing I can THINK of.

Food - snacks - treats...

I really want MY story to get into the book.
What can I write about that Mr Fullerman
will give me FIVE STARS for?

I'm trying to remember OTHER FUNNY STORIES
I have. Some I probably shouldn't write about.
Like the time I drew a picture of
Mr Fullerbum on the back of my
homework (accidentally).

Mr Fullerbum

OR when I called Mrs Worthington
"Mum" by mistake, and she saw the EXTREME
close-up picture I drew of her.

I got a detention for that.

<---- EXTREME CLOSE-UP

Oh ... and the time I drew Mr Keen's eyebrows as caterpillars.

I'm not sure I'd get FIVE STARS for any of
☆☆☆☆☆
those ideas.

thinking
face

At break time, I ask around to see what everyone else is going to write about.

"I might do a story about Rooster – he's ALWAYS doing something FUNNY," Derek tells me.

(True.)

Leroy tells us a story about his dad, who used to pretend that money could come out of his **EARS** like ☆**MAGIC**☆

 "I believed him for **AGES!**" Leroy says.

"Does it have to be a REAL story?" Florence asks.

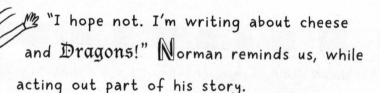 "I hope not. I'm writing about cheese and **Dragons!**" Norman reminds us, while acting out part of his story.

Everyone seems to have good 😊 ideas for their stories apart from ME.

"You'll think of something, Tom," Derek assures me. I hope so.

Ideas... Ideas...

Even when school's finished and I'm walking home,
I'm still trying to think of story ideas. But I don't
know **what** I can write about.
My mind's gone **BLANK**. I wish I could get some
INSPIRATION from somewhere?

But nothing's happening.

When I get home, I go straight to the kitchen to check the fridge. Delia's already there so I STOP. She's obviously not going to move, so I decide to ask her a question.

"Oh..."

"Delia, Deeelia."

"What do you want, Tom?"

"If you had to write a **FUNNY STORY**, what would you write about?"

"Let me think... I know! Your school photos always make me **LAUGH**," she says.

"Very **FUNNY**." I sigh.

"Yes, they are." Delia smiles.

Delia sort of smiling

Then she says...

"Why don't you go and look in your room for inspiration, Tom? You might find something FUNNY up there."

 I know Delia is trying to get rid of me, but it's not such a bad idea.

"Or take a look in the mirror. That might give you an idea for a FUNNY STORY," she says.

 "Ha ha, you're HILARIOUS."

 "I know. Thanks, Tom."

I go to my room and have a look around at all my collections. Like my stone collection.

holes in stones

dog

stone looks
like a foot

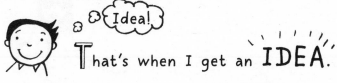

That's when I get an IDEA.

I could write a FUNNY story about HOW I got this stone. It's my special stone and I bring it everywhere with me (if I remember to).

But then again ...

... there's always

Great-Aunt Aggie's fake bird hat.

I keep it on top of my wardrobe so the fake birds look down at me.

Maybe I should write about how <u>I</u> got the hat?

(Suddenly, I'm getting LOTS of good ideas.)

The hat used to belong to Granddad Bob's *Great-Aunt Aggie*. I've seen pictures of her wearing it, and she looked

FIERCE.

 elia thinks the hat is creepy.

 "It's not creepy. Granddad says it's **LUCKY**," I told her.

"Not for those birds it wasn't," Delia said.

 "They're **FAKE** birds, not real birds," I reminded her.

If Granddad ever asks Mum about the hat, she gets it down so Granddad can see we're looking after it.
This hat **COULD** be a good story for the book.
But would it be **FUNNY** enough to get me

☆ **FIVE STARS** ? (Maybe.)

It all started when Mum and Dad got an invitation to a party...

One day a *posh*-looking envelope dropped through our letter box. It had a red wax seal on the back and the address was written in very *fancy* handwriting. I gave it to Mum, who was excited to open it.

"What's that?" I asked.

YES!

"Something special, I hope," Mum said.

I've never seen her JUMP up and down like that about a letter.

"Have we won the **LOTTERY?**" I asked.

"No, Tom – I think we've been invited to a super *fancy* party," she told me.

"BRILLIANT! I LOVE parties!" I said.

Brilliant!

"Sorry, Tom, no kids allowed."

 "Huh?" This was a **SHOCK.**

"Why can't I come?"

"It's just for grown-ups. You wouldn't enjoy it anyway," Mum tried to explain. (I might.)

Mum took the invitation to show Dad, who was outside working in the shed, leaving the envelope behind. I picked it up for a closer look and noticed there was a small card inside.

It said ⟨ THE DRESS CODE ⟩ on one side. There was NOTHING about kids not being allowed.

"Are you SURE I can't come?" I checked when Mum and Dad came back in.

 "Totally sure. You might have to stay with Granny and Granddad as Delia's going out that night. That's OK, isn't it?" Mum asked, checking the calendar on the fridge.

$\mathbb{I}$ always have a nice time with **THE FOSSILS** (that's what I call my grandparents, in case you don't know). Dad seemed **EXCITED** about the party as well.

I can't remember the last time we were invited to a big posh do like this.

I know!

"You'll have to get something smarter to wear," Mum told him.

And I'm not sure you'll be able to wear that hat, either.

"**W**hat's wrong with my old suit, and that T-shirt with the BOW TIE drawn on, these trainers and my hat, Rita?" Dad asked seriously before he started to **LAUGH**.

"Don't worry – I'm still wearing the hat, though," he added.

Mum wasn't smiling.

I knew the party must be a **BIG** deal when Dad hired a SUIT and then told Uncle Kevin and Aunty Alice all about the invite when they popped round.

"Wait, you're going to *THAT* party?" Uncle Kevin said, in a very surprised way.

"Yes, we are. Didn't you get an invitation?" Dad smiled.

"We did, but we can't go. We're busy."

"You might be busy, but I'm not," Aunty Alice muttered.

(I think Aunty Alice really wanted to go to the party.)

TOP SUITS

☺ ⟵ furious

When Delia heard about the *fancy* PARTY,
the first thing she said was,
"I'm not babysitting. I've got PLANS."

"I'm staying at Granny and Granddad's ... AND
I'm not a baby," I said quickly so she couldn't
grumble at me. It's not *FUN* for anyone when
Delia babysits - especially ME.

Bedtime, Tom.

But it's only six o'clock and it's still light.

On the night of the party, Mum and Dad took AGES to get ready. I'd packed a bag EARLY with all the IMPORTANT stuff like my 🪨 stone collection and comics. Mum and Dad were going to

TREAT us to a takeaway so Granny Mavis didn't have to cook anything ODD with bits in.

← bits

It was getting later and later and I was still waiting when Mum called out:

Dad didn't answer at first. He was too busy dancing in front of the mirror.

FRANK! Don't forget to bring the invitation. We need it to get into the party!

"What do you think, Tom?" he asked me. "The suit's better than your dancing, Dad," I pointed out. He tilted his hat in different directions to check which looked best.

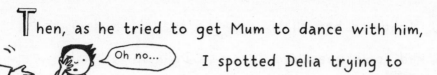 hen, as he tried to get Mum to dance with him, **Oh no...** I spotted Delia trying to sneak out of the house.

Obviously, I shouted,

 # MUM, DAD, DELIA'S GOING OUT!

"Message us when you get home and don't be late," Mum told her. **I will.**

Dad showed her a few of his dance moves, which made Delia leave even faster.

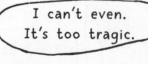 I can't even. It's too tragic.

I followed her all the way to the front door and asked some questions (because Delia loves that).

"Where EXACTLY are you going?"

"Do you like wafers more than cakes?"

"What time are you coming home?"

"Don't you like dancing?"

"What would you rather do, swim with sharks, or sit in a tree with a bear?"

"Why didn't you want to say goodbye?"

BYE!

BYE, TOM.

BYE!

BYE, DELIA!

I waved goodbye to her. It was like she couldn't get away fast enough.

Dad stopped dancing and carried my overnight bag to the car.

"What have you got in here? It weighs a TON."

"Just all the IMPORTANT things I need," I explained.

"Like your pyjamas?" Dad checked.

I had to run back and get them.

"And your toothbrush!" he called.

(I had to go back for that too.)

Normally, if I'm staying the night somewhere, Mum and Dad fuss a LOT more. But they were both in such a **GOOD MOOD** they even let me choose the music in the car. We had a nice singsong all the way to **THE FOSSILS'** house.

We even sat in the car until the song finished.

Are we nearly there yet?

Granny Mavis was wondering why we took so long to get out of the car.

"Don't you all look FANTASTIC!"

she told us as we walked inside.

I said,  even though I wasn't going to the party.

"They all scrub up well! Just like me!"

Granddad added.

Mum and Dad thanked for having me and then said they needed to leave.

"I've been told latecomers get the worst seats," Dad said.

Granny was being very organized and called them a taxi. Then Mum checked again...

"You **did** bring the $\boxed{invitation}$, Frank, didn't you?"

Dad enjoyed patting his pockets, looking for a bit longer than he should have done.

(It was under his hat.)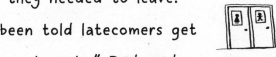

Tah-dah!

"As if I'd forget the invitation, Rita!"
Dad smiled.

"Did you know your GALA DINNER was
in the local paper? Apparently, there'll be lots
of VERY IMPORTANT people there,"
Granny said, taking a look at the invitation.

OAKFIELD
GAZETTE
Important
people Rita
and Frank
go to gala
party.

"Important people LIKE US,"
Dad added, and Mum
 rolled her eyes.

They both gave me a hug as the taxi arrived.
"Be good, Tom!" Mum said as she headed out the door.

NO! YOU CAN'T GO!

I shouted dramatically, which made them STOP.

"WHAT'S WRONG?" Dad said.

"It's only one night," Mum added.

"Granny's got your invitation!"
I passed it over and a small
card fell on the floor.

"What's that?" Dad asked.

"It's just the dress code card,"
                            I said and picked it up.

Dress code: this year's theme is hats.
Please dress smartly and WEAR A HAT.
There will be a photographer on
the night.

Mum froze.

"HATS? HATS?
WHAT HATS?"

she said.

Mum kept saying the word "HATS" like she didn't know what a hat was.

"Where am I going to get a hat NOW?" she asked in a panic.

Dad pointed to his own hat and suggested, "Hey, we can share mine. No one will notice." he popped it on Mum's head.

I'll ask the taxi to wait...

Then I had an IDEA. I pointed to the pegs. "Mum, you could wear one of THOSE hats!"

"Good thinking, Tom!" Dad went to grab a selection.

"You're welcome to wear any of our hats, Rita," Granddad told her.
This was a HAT EMERGENCY after all.

"Try this." Dad gave Mum the first hat.

"If you turn it round, it won't say BOB on the front," I pointed out.

"I can't wear a bobble hat to a gala dinner. No offence, Bob."

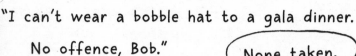

None taken.

Mum was trying not to get stressed and tried on the other hats as quickly as she could.

Dad said the flat cap looked "edgy".

Mum didn't agree.

Nope.

The straw boater was too big and had holes in it.

"I can make a paper hat for you, Mum!" I suggested.

"Thanks, Tom, but I'm not sure that's going to work." Mum and Dad were going to be REALLY late if they didn't leave soon.

"There's not enough time to go home, and all the shops are closed," Dad announced.

"That's really HELPFUL, Frank." Mum wasn't impressed. We were all thinking of what to do when Granddad shouted,

CREAK

"RITA! I've GOT IT!

Why didn't I think of this before? My *Great-Aunt Aggie's* hat's been in the family for years. I'll go and get it - it's PERFECT!"

"Bob, you're a ★STAR★, thank you!

We might even make it to the party on time now!" Mum sounded relieved.

Granddad *rushed* off to get it as fast as he could go.

(Which wasn't very fast.)

S L O W   M O T I O N

Eventually, Granddad reappeared holding a
SMART HAT BOX.

"That's such a GREAT IDEA, Bob! You've wanted to pass that hat down for ages," Granny reminded him. "And the taxi's still waiting," she added.

Mum took the box quickly.
"Bob, this is AMAZING. I'm going to wear *Great-Aunt Aggie's* hat with PRIDE."

Then she opened the box...

Mum was struggling to speak, so I asked, "Are they REAL BIRDS?"

"NO! They're FAKE. *Aunt Aggie* hand sewed everything on to the hat. It took her a very long time. Let me help you put it on, Rita. It's a very precious hat," Granddad said and helped her try it on.

It sounded like the hat meant a LOT to Granddad. The birds did look pretty impressive.

Then Mum put the hat on ...

... and disappeared under the brim.

"Oh no ... it's far too big," Mum called from underneath. We could only see her mouth moving. "I need something to pad it out inside, lift the hat up a bit. Frank, can you help?" Mum asked.

"Don't move, Rita. I've got this."
Dad ran into the kitchen and came back holding ...

Huh?

 ... two rolls of kitchen paper, which didn't seem like the best idea to me (or Mum).

"Don't panic. Take the hat off," Dad said and started to STUFF the inside of the hat with paper.

"You've got a really tiny head, Rita," he commented. "Let's see if this works."

Mum put the hat back on and with a few more pieces of kitchen roll, the hat fit perfectly (sort of).

 "It really suits you, Rita. This hat was MEANT for you. It's been in the box far too long. I'm so glad you can wear it to such a lovely event. You must keep the hat. It's YOURS," Granddad told Mum proudly.

"I couldn't possibly, Bob. The hat belongs in your family."

"You *are* my family, Rita," Granddad reminded Mum.

Dad was tapping his watch. "We'd better go..."

"I'll just have a quick look in the mirror."

"Make sure you can't see the kitchen roll – that wouldn't be..."

"Oh MY GIDDY AUNT..."

Mum said slowly, which didn't make sense because I thought the hat was *Great-Aunt Aggie's?*

"Think of the party, Rita. You're a TWEET for the eyes," Dad said and LAUGHED.

 and I stood at the door and WAVED
Mum and Dad off.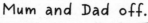

BRING BACK NICE TREATS,
PLEASE! LIKE CAKE!

(All good parties have cake, don't they?)

"When I saw your mum wearing that hat, all these memories came flooding back."

Granddad sighed.

"Aww, that's nice, Bob." Granny smiled.

"Can I watch TV and go to bed really late?"

I asked hopefully.

Granddad carried on chatting like he wasn't really listening.

So I said it again and this time added in **SNACKS**.

"Can I watch TV, go to bed really late AND eat snacks?"

 "Ooh! Snacks. I've got just the thing for us to have, Tom,"

Granny said.

(Oh...)

Even though Granny might have made odd snacks, this was still going to be an EXCELLENT evening.

I got to choose a film, which was EASY.

SWAMP MONSTER

(Not like at home when we can never

agree what to watch.) 😕

Then Granny ordered pizza while Granddad showed

me some old photos of *Great-Aunt Aggie.*

"She was always the life and soul of the party,"

he said.

(It was hard to believe from the photos.)

We had the **BEST** evening ever watching the film, eating pizza and staying up late (ish).
SWAMP MONSTER 1 was a big hit.
Granny even asked about watching **SWAMP MONSTER 2.**
"Is it as good as this one?" she wondered.

It's the same.

(True.)

In the end I didn't stay up too late and all the IMPORTANT stuff I'd packed in my case (COMICS, interesting stones, teddy) all helped me get to sleep.

That night I had a dream about
a **SWAMP MONSTER ...**

... who was wearing a hat made of CAKE.

So the **SWAMP MONSTERS** ate it.

In the morning, Granny called me down for breakfast nice and late.  I was very RELAXED until I saw the pot of STURDY porridge she'd made (with bits in).

Delicious.

"No thanks, Granny."

I found some choco pops instead and had those.

CHOCO POPS

"I hope your mum and dad had a nice time last night," Granny said.

"And I hope *Great-Aunt Aggie's* hat was a big SUCCESS," Granddad added.

"We'll find out soon. They're here already," Granny said as the doorbell rang. DING DONG!

"Awwwwwwwwwwwww ...

do I have to go? We could watch ."

"Maybe next time, Tom." Granddad smiled.
I went to get dressed and collect up all my stuff.

When I came down, Mum and Dad were chatting
about the party and wanted to know
how my evening was.

"TOM! Did you have *FUN*?"

"You didn't keep anyone up snoring, did you?"
Dad LAUGHED.

Granddad wanted to know all about

Great-Aunt Aggie's hat.

"Was the hat a HUGE SUCCESS? Did everyone love it?"

"Everyone loved the hat, Bob."

"You can say that again," Dad said.

"It was the talk of the party."

"Yes, it was..." Mum agreed.

"And how about the **CAKE**?" I asked as that was an
important question.

No one answered my cake question.

"What were the OTHER hats like?"

Granddad asked.

"Very different to Aunt Aggie's."

Mum LAUGHED.

"It was definitely **THE** most talked about hat on

the night."

 "Did anyone talk about 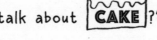?"

I tried again.

"How about photos? Did anyone take pictures

of you wearing the hat, Rita?"

Granddad wanted to know.

"It wasn't that kind of party. Sorry, Bob,"

Mum explained.

"Was it the kind of party that had CAKE?" I asked.

(Still no answer...)

"What a shame. I'd have loved to have seen you wearing the hat in such a fancy setting, Rita." Granddad sounded a bit sad.

 "I'd have LOVED to have seen the CAKE," I added, doing my best.

"Maybe there'll be another party I can wear the hat to?" Mum told Granddad.

"Are you sure about that?" Dad whispered.

"Another party that has CAKE!" I added a bit louder.

Then Granny suddenly said, "HEY! Why don't you ALL come to the **MUSIC NIGHT PARTY** at the LEAFY GREEN OLD FOLKS' HOME? Everyone's going to be dressing up for that. You can wear the hat again, Rita!"

"Oh ... I suppose I could,"

Mum told Granny.

"Really?" Dad asked.

Mum and Dad didn't sound very enthusiastic about another party.

But I **WAS!**

"Can I come and will there be CAKE?" I checked.

"Yes, Tom, there'll be cake and bow ties, hats and lots of ♫MUSIC.♫ Of course you can come," Granny said.

"Tea Cup Tony says he'll make a SPECIAL effort to join in the FUN. It's going to be GREAT," Granddad added.

I can't wait for the CAKE! And the bird hat, of course!

"Looks like we're going to another party then," Dad said.

Mum didn't seem so excited.

I spotted she was holding what looked like two boxes of ... CAKE?

Is that CAKE?

I shouted.

"It might be. Go and get your bag. Then you can have some."

This made me hurry up.

(I am very snack driven.)

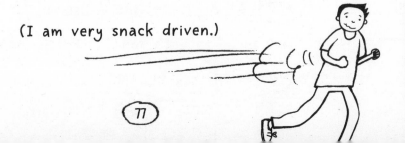

I'd put all my old stones (and some new ones I'd found) in my bag, then said BYE and thank you to THE FOSSILS. "See you at the music party!" Dad complained about my bag being **heavy** (again) as he put it in the car.

On the journey home, I asked the important questions. "Will I need to wear a hat at the LEAFY GREEN party?"

"Maybe. Can you wear the bird hat again, Rita?" Dad asked Mum.

"As long as there are no cats around." Mum LAUGHED.

When Mum and Dad both say "NOTHING" together, I know something is going on.

Especially as they let me eat my cake in the car.

Which was fine by me, but suspicious. (Normally they don't like the crumbs.) Dad was still grumbling about my **heavy** bag as he took it upstairs.

I changed the subject and asked, "Is there any more CAKE?"

"You've had your piece, Tom. Why don't you unpack your bag?" Dad suggested.

Looking for more CAKE seemed like a better idea.

Walking past Mum and Dad's bedroom I SPOTTED *Great-Aunt Aggie's* bird hat on a table.

The hat looked different – and NOT

in a good way...

WHAT HAPPENED TO
Great-Aunt Aggie's HAT?

Granddad wouldn't be happy about this. I picked up the hat (carefully) and took it downstairs.

"Mum! DAD! THE BIRD HAT'S ALL CRUSHED AND WONKY!"

I shouted.

Mum looked surprised.

"TOM! Don't drop it and make it WORSE!"

(Like that was possible.)

"What happened to the hat, Mum?"

"Nothing I can't fix, Tom. Pass it over. I've
got the sewing box ready, and Granddad doesn't
need to know, OK?" she said.

"Know what? What did you do?" I asked, as
I was confused.

"It wasn't ME, Tom. Your dad will explain."

"Dad did it?" I asked.

"NO, I SAVED the hat from looking even WORSE.
The CAT did it," Dad said.

"Why was there a cat at the party?"
THIS I had to hear!

Dad tried to explain while Mum tried to fix the hat. Turns out the cat lives at the fancy house where the gala party was being held. (Lucky cat.)

1

The cat saw the birds on Mum's hat from the staircase.

2

It was hungry and waited for the right moment to ...

3 POUNCE on

TOP OF the hat that

Mum was still wearing.

There was a BIG SCENE.

The cat MEOWED and tried to eat the birds.
Mum shouted, "GET OFF!" and shook her head,
which made the cat

CLING ON EVEN MORE!

The birds got badly BASHED UP and bits of
kitchen roll fell out. There were feathers everywhere
until Mum managed to shake the cat to the floor.

IT WAS CHAOS!

(I wish I'd been there to see it!)

This sounded like THE MOST EXCITING PARTY EVER.

(And the **CAKE** was delicious too.)

"I need to repair the hat right NOW, Tom. I can't let Granddad see his beloved hat looking like **THIS**," Mum told me.

"Won't Granddad see the hat at the LEAFY GREEN **Music Night** PARTY?" I wondered.

"I hope not. The hat will be fine by then," Mum said.

"I just HOPE they don't hear about the cat from someone else," Dad added.

"And if they do, at least there were no photos as evidence. That's something," he said before Delia came in holding the latest copy of the local paper and smiling.

"Have you seen the front page of the **Oakfield Gazette?** It's a good headline."

Delia held it up, to Mum and Dad's surprise.

"Oh no."

"Oh..."

OAKFIELD GAZETTE
It's a HAT
CATastrophe!

"Mum, you're **FAMOUS.**

Or the cat is," I said.

"Oh no. **THE FOSSILS** will SEE this and think I've ruined their precious hat!"

 "What are you going to do?" I asked.

"The only thing we can," Mum told me.

 "Tell Granddad EXACTLY what happened?" I said.

"Not yet..."

Mum and Dad were hoping  wouldn't SPOT the **headline** in the paper before the hat was fixed.

While Mum fixed *Great-Aunt Aggie's bird hat,* Dad went out to get as MANY papers as he could. It took him a while and we ended up with a LOT of papers in our house.

I was looking forward to the

LEAFY GREEN **MUSIC NIGHT PARTY.**

I wore my sunglasses, my T-shirt, but no hat.

(I'd leave that to Mum and .)

The **MUSIC NIGHT** was a **BIG** success. ☺

Everybody in the LEAFY GREEN OLD FOLKS'

HOME managed to dress up. Vera wore a

FASCINATOR which was fascinating with its long

feathers.

Tea Cup Tony had a top hat and sang his classic

song (A nice cup of tea! ♪ ♫)

before heading for a nap. zzzz zzz

Granny and Granddad were DELIGHTED

to see Mum wearing *Great-Aunt Aggie's bird*

hat. Mum had done <u>such</u> a good job of repairing

the birds, plumping and sewing things back together,

that no one noticed anything different about it. The

hat looked almost like it did before...

Almost...

(Just don't look too closely at the birds' eyes.)

The **CAKE** was PERFECT, though.

I really hope Mr Fullerman will give me five stars
for this story. ★★★★★

Now every morning when I wake up I can see 👀
the wonky birds 🐦🐦 and they make me LAUGH.
Hopefully Mr Fullerman will LAUGH too.

I do have other things to write about ...

... like my stone collection.

Some stones I keep in boxes and others I put on display or take them with me when I go out.

weird stones

Derek and I try to find stones that look like other things. I like to paint and draw on them as well. They make good presents for people.

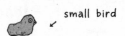

small bird

Delia's got quite a few now.

Is it another painted stone? You shouldn't have.

It's a present.

Sometimes she jams them up against her door to stop me from barging into her room.

(It doesn't always work.)

I'm HERE!

"Brilliant..."

CLUNK

This stone is from my "STONE with a HOLE IN" collection.  I've drawn on one side of it, and every time I think about how I found it, I LAUGH.

If **ONLY** there was a funny story about a **STONE** in this book. I could give it five stars...

This could happen.

Here's my stone-with-a-hole-in story.

At school I did a SHOW AND TELL for my class all about my stone collection, which seemed to start a BIG CRAZE on STONES. (These things happen.)

This stone looks just like Mr Fullerman, especially the EYES.

Ahem?

Lots of kids went looking for interesting stones at break time. Caretaker Stan had to ask everyone to

"Stop digging up the flower beds to find stones!"

The STONE CRAZE became so popular that Mrs Mumble even made an announcement over the loudspeaker to say:

"PLEASE DON'T collect STONES from the school grounds, or there will be NONE left! Thank you!"

But now THE WHOLE ENTIRE SCHOOL knew about the and it felt like EVERYBODY wanted to join in.

Stones were being traded like marbles, and you could always SPOT someone who had a LARGE stone collection from the way they carried their school bag.

In class Marcus kept showing me and **AMY** what he thought was a really interesting stone.

"What do you think this one looks like?" he asked.

"A stone," I answered.

"You know what I mean.

What do you think it is, **AMY**?"

"Give me a clue."

"Isn't it OBVIOUS?"

"Errr, not really," **AMY** and I told Marcus.

I didn't know and neither did **AMY**.

Marcus got annoyed that we couldn't guess it.

"It's an AARDVARK*, of course!"

"What does an AARDVARK look like?"

I asked, and Marcus showed me the stone again.

"Like THIS!" he said.

"Like a STONE?"   "Oh, never mind..."

*See page 224 for an aardvark picture!

Here's a chart I made of the BEST stones to find.

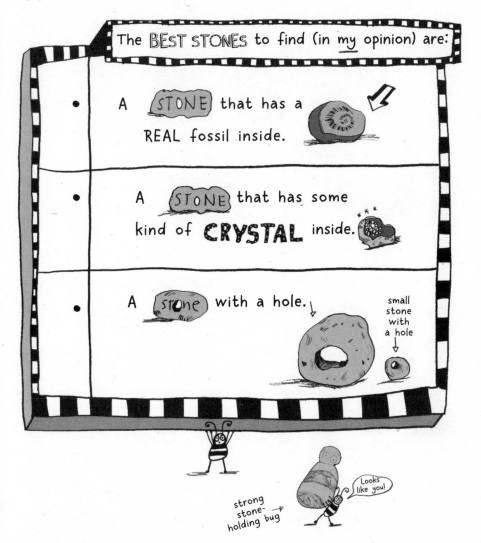

The BEST STONES to find (in my opinion) are:

- A STONE that has a REAL fossil inside.

- A STONE that has some kind of CRYSTAL inside.

- A stone with a hole.

small stone with a hole

strong stone-holding bug

Looks like you!

The only STONE I was missing to complete my stone with a HOLE collection was a BIG one.

tiny

medium

missing

Derek and I had been looking for AGES, but we hadn't managed to find the EXACT-size stone with a hole in.

THEN Mr Fullerman announced we were all going on a SCHOOL TRIP. He said we'd all be taking part in Pick Up Plastic Week and going to a LAKE!

This was EXCITING NEWS for lots of different reasons (mostly because LAKES = LOADS OF STONES).

I'd be able to find EXACTLY the right stone. It would be so much easier by a LAKE, wouldn't it?

(YES.)

happy face

The stone craze in school was still going on, so I knew that stone competition would be FIERCE.

MINE!

BUT I wasn't going to worry about it.

Hopefully there would be enough to go around.

STONES!

FOUND SOME!

On the day of the school **Pick Up Plastic Week** trip, I was a bit late (Uh-oh!) because I'd spent too long trying to decide which STONES I should bring with me. I needed to compare sizes and find the PERFECT stone to add to my collection. Just to be on the safe side I brought a few in my bag to compare.

 "Your bag looks **heavy**, Tom. What have you got in there?" Dad asked.

"All the important stuff for the trip," I told him.

Dad gave me a lift to school so I didn't miss the coach. I was the last kid to arrive, running with my heavy bag.

clunk
clunk

 **"COME ON, TOM, HURRY UP AND TAKE A SEAT!"** Mr Fullerman called out.

puff puff

Normally Derek would have saved me a seat next to him, but his class are doing this trip on a different day. The only seat left was next to ...

clunk

clunk

... Julia Morton.

She was already holding a sick bag.

"This is for EMERGENCY only, Tom.
I'm much better at travelling now," Julia assured me.
Once the coach set off,  Julia was fine.
I was the one who felt ill.

All that swerving around and STOP ...

➡ START was making me feel properly QUEASY.

"Here, take this..." Julia handed me the bag.

It wasn't a good start to the trip.

I managed to hold it together until we arrived at the lake and got off the coach. (Phew!)

Mr Fullerman saw the colour of my face and asked, **"Are you OK, Tom? Take some deep breaths of FRESH AIR and you'll feel better."**

So I did.

It was working until Norman offered me one of his **PICKLED ONION** snacks.

Normally I'd LOVE one, but the smell wasn't helping.

"You must feel bad if you don't want a snack," Norman noted.

"I'll be fine," I said and breathed some more.

Mr Fullerman gathered us all around and said, **"Isn't it great, Class 5F, to be by the lake in the lovely fresh air and SUN."**

Just then it started to rain ... a LOT.

I looked around at all my classmates who were
wearing waterproof coats and were nice and dry –
not like me.

"You <u>did</u> bring SOMETHING WATERPROOF to wear, didn't you, Tom?"
Mr Fullerman asked.

"Not really..." I said.

Holding a piece of paper over my head wasn't working.

Mrs Mumble came to my rescue with the spare clothes bag.

"I don't have a coat, Tom, but I'll see what else we can find for you."

Mrs Mumble brought out what looked like a blanket and a small umbrella.

"It's not ideal; the blanket is for picnics, but it's waterproof and will keep you dry," she told me.

"And this might work too," she added.

Mrs Mumble put the blanket round my should
like a cloak and then opened up a really small
umbrella and put it ... ON MY HEAD LIKE A HAT!

"It's better than getting soaking wet, Tom," she
told me, as the rain bounced off the umbrella hat.

Marcus made a special effort to come over and tell me,

"You look ridiculous."

"At least I'm keeping DRY,"
        I replied.

Which was true until Norman
jumped in a puddle and my legs got soaking wet.

"Sorry, Tom. Nice umbrella hat, though," Norman said.

Mr Fullerman took us to meet the **Pick Up Plastic Week** crew who were waiting for us under a shelter.

"HELLO, Class 5F from Oakfield School. We are so happy you've joined us today to be part of our **Pick Up Plastic** campaign," the lady said cheerily. "My name is YELLOW. Before you ask, that IS my real name."

(Marcus already had his hand up.)

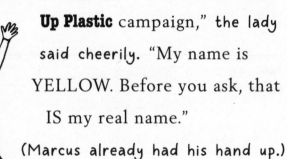

"And my name is SONNY, or Son for short. So together we're Yellow and Son."

They both waved at us enthusiastically.

We waved back just as enthusiastically.

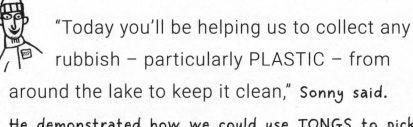

"Today you'll be helping us to collect any rubbish – particularly PLASTIC – from around the lake to keep it clean," Sonny said.
He demonstrated how we could use TONGS to pick up the plastic.

"We'll give you gloves and you should use the tongs for anything you want to pick up," Yellow said.
"Don't use your hands and make sure you wear the gloves. Put all the plastic in these bins."

"We can all do that, can't we, Class 5F?"
Mr Fullerman aked.

"YES!"

We were excited.
None of us could WAIT to try out the tongs ...

... **on** each other.

Mr Fullerman put a stop to our fun with his

STARE OF DOOM. - - - -

**"Everyone, follow Yellow and Sonny to the
lake, please,"** he said firmly.

"Tom, hurry up. You don't need your bag."

(I <u>did</u> need a stone from my bag to help me find
the <u>**PERFECT**</u> sized stone for my collection, so
I grabbed one and put it in my pocket.)

Marcus (nosy parker) wanted to know why I was bringing a stone with me.

 "I'm looking for the next size up from this stone to complete my collection," I said. "A lake is a good place for that."

"You're SUPPOSED to be looking for plastic, not stones, Tom," Marcus told me (smugly).

"I can do both." I smiled.

But as we got closer to the water, I could see my stone-collecting plans might not be so easy.

"Oh dear, Tom, not many stones on all this **grass**. Bad luck," Marcus enjoyed telling me.

I was going to try even harder now.

With our tongs at the ready, my class set off in the rain to clear up any plastic or rubbish from the (VERY) grassy and non-stony lake.

It wasn't long before I was expertly picking up  bottle tops, torn plastic bags, lolly sticks and a few other bits and pieces.

It felt good to be doing something useful.

All the time, though, I kept my eyes OPEN for excellent stones.

I was starting to think this was going to be impossible when

SOMETHING CAUGHT MY EYE.

It might be a stone. It was slightly hidden under some weeds, so I moved closer for a better LOOK and noticed the stone was SPARKLING.

Could it be?

Was it?

Stone number two on my list.

A stone with a CRYSTAL in it.

This was EXCITING!

I didn't want to bring too much attention to the stone. I tried to *relax* and casually move nearer with my TONGS at the ready to pick it up.

When a GUST OF WIND WHISKED THE UMBRELLA HAT OFF MY HEAD.

I chased it along the ground and grabbed it with my tongs. Then I put it back on quickly.

AGH! By the time I got back to

MY stone ...

... it had G**O**NE and ...

(Oh.)

AMY was holding it.

"Look at this stone I found, Tom. It's AMAZING. It was just under that bit of weed. I've always wanted a stone like this."

"Yeah ... me too." I sighed.

"I can't believe I saw it sparkling. I never thought stones were that interesting until I saw your collection," **AMY** said.

I tried to be pleased for her.

"I can't believe you saw it either." Marcus came over to have a look.

"Did you find that stone, Tom?"

"No, I did," **AMY** replied.

"Bad luck, Tom," Marcus said.

"I'm going to keep looking. There <u>MUST</u> be more stones by this lake," I told Marcus.

"Good idea. I want to find a stone like that too."

I pretended not to care that Marcus
        wanted to join in.

Fine...

Good luck.

(But I did.)

Mr Fullerman pointed to the ground, which was code for **"get back to picking up plastic"**.

"Look, sir, I've found a stone with a crystal in it!" **AMY** said and everyone gathered round to see the glittery stone.

"EXCELLENT, Amy. You're <u>all</u> doing a fantastic job. Keep it up!"

I decided to go in a different direction to Marcus, and was determined <u>NOT</u> to get distracted by anything this time. I was going to find my PERFECT (STONE).

Using my tongs, I looked under weeds, checked behind rocks and kept my eyes peeled.

Solid came over to join me. He was holding a plastic bottle to put in the bin. "I like using these tongs, don't you?" he asked.

"Yes! Although I'm trying to find interesting stones for my collection as well. I haven't found anything yet. It's not **that** easy by a lake, is it?" I said to Solid.

"I don't know, Tom. Look what I found over there." Solid took a flat stone from his pocket ...

... with what looked like a **FOSSIL** inside.

"I've never found anything like this before.
It's great, isn't it?" Solid said.

I WAS (ALMOST) SPEECHLESS!

Yes, it is...
That looks like a **FOSSIL** in
the stone, Solid.

"I thought so. I'm going to add it to my
collection. I only started collecting
stones after your show and tell. Thanks, Tom."

"No problem, Solid." I sighed.
"Where did you find it again?" I asked.

"Over there, just where Marcus is standing,"
Solid told me.   (Brilliant.)

Should I go over and join Marcus,

or look in another place?

Finding a **FOSSIL** would be AMAZING. I took a risk.

And I joined Marcus.

As SOON as he saw me, he said,

"Solid found a stone with a **FOSSIL** in it."

"I know."

"That's what I'm looking for," he added.

"Me too."

We both got busy trying to find anything that resembled a stone. Marcus wasn't going to get one before me, not this time. But it wasn't easy. We got in each other's way picking up what we both thought were stones.

"I saw it first..." I told him.

"HEY, that was mine..."
Marcus kept saying,
which was annoying.

I let Marcus take what I could see was a bottle top. I'd spotted something right by his foot that looked VERY promising. I glanced down quickly and could see it was a STONE! Not just any old stone, but what looked like the EXACT SIZE I needed to complete my COLLECTION!

While Marcus kept on talking about Solid's **FOSSIL**, I tried my best to move my tongs closer to the stone without Marcus noticing. Slowly ... slowly ... slowly...

Until Marcus only went and STOOD right on top of the stone.

"What's that?" he said and lifted his foot up to take a look.

"It's NOTHING!" I shouted.

"Doesn't look like nothing to me..."

"HEY! It's my LUCKY DAY. Look, Tom, I've found this STONE with a hole. I've started collecting these stones since your show and tell. It's not a FOSSIL, but I'm going to KEEP IT,"

Marcus told me excitedly.

Awww no!

"That's EXACTLY the size of stone I was looking for," I said, hoping Marcus might give it to me.

(No chance.)

Marcus enjoyed waving the stone out of my reach.

"I wouldn't do that if I were you," I said.

"It's MY stone now." Marcus LAUGHED. He knew I collected those stones.

"Marcus, there's a seagull flying towards you and it thinks you've got FOOD," I tried to explain.

"Yeah, right, Tom. Like I'm going to fall for that," he said smugly before...

The seagull swooped down and grabbed the stone and flew off.

Not food.

AGH!

Marcus yelped,

"AGH! That's MINE! Mr Fullerman, a seagull took my STONE!" he yelped.

Marcus was so busy shouting and running away that he didn't see the seagull DROP the stone out of its mouth.

BUT I did... And I saw where it landed too. I quickly picked up the stone and kept it safely under my blanket. The rain even stopped and the sun came out.

Result!

Things were really looking up for me.

"But was the seagull OK?" Mr Fullerman

checked. He didn't seem that worried about Marcus.

"It was the biggest seagull ever," "SIR?"

Marcus exaggerated.

It was time for us to stop collecting, and Sonny and

Yellow congratulated everyone on all our hard work.

"Great job, Oakfield School, you've all worked so

hard collecting up the rubbish and plastic."

 And stones, I was thinking.

Mrs Mumble took back my umbrella hat and

blanket, which was pretty wet.

"Wasn't it useful? I might get one

for myself," she said.

I popped my NEW stone with a hole into

my bag before Marcus saw it. I was looking forward

to getting home and adding it to my collection.

still grumpy

I wasn't the only one.

"I'm so HAPPY I found this crystal stone!" AMY told the class as we ate our packed lunches.

"My **FOSSIL** stone is the BEST thing I've EVER found!" Solid said.

"SIR, did I tell you my stone with a hole in got pinched by a bird?" Marcus wanted to SHARE.

"You did, Marcus." Mr Fullerman sighed.

"Your class are very into collecting things," Yellow noted.

"I think it's a school trend. It's stones this week and pencil rubbers the next!" Mr Fullerman explained. (He could be right.) Sitting next to Julia on the coach back home, she did have a pencil with an excellent face on a rubber at the end. (I could collect them!)

Hello!

The first thing I did when I got home was to get out all my stones with holes and arrange them in size order. My new stone fit in perfectly and looking at the stone's shape, it really reminded me of something.

my new stone fit perfectly

I used my special pen and drew a face on the stone. Now it will ALWAYS remind me of going on the **Pick Up Plastic** school trip and all the funny things that happened.

Here is Marcus Meldrew when he ignored my warning and the bird pinched his stone.

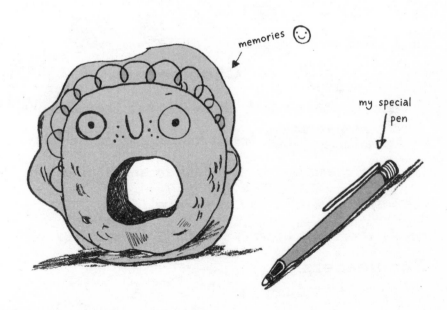

memories 🙂

my special pen

Looking at my stone makes me LAUGH. Ha! Ha! Ha! Ha!
Ha!
Ha! Ha! Ha! Ha! Ha! Ha!

I hope Mr Fullerman will find it funny and
★ ★ ★ ★ ★
immediately give me FIVE STARS for this story.

Space for stars:

Or I could write about my EMPTY box of

Chocteezers.

I know it doesn't look like much, but they are one

of my FAVOURITE treats to have in the cinema.

They are chocolate on the outside and caramel on

the inside. I wish I had some now.

Here's the story of why I kept this empty box of

Chocteezers.

choc

caramel
inside

I got THIS BOX at the **CINEMA CLUB** with Derek and my friends.

Derek had to remind me we were going with a **BIG** sign at his bedroom window that said

Then he followed it up with this sign about jelly snakes.

I gave him the thumbs up and wrote a quick sign myself.

Leroy and **N**orman were meeting us at the **CINEMA** with DIFFERENT snacks, so the sooner we got there the BETTER.

Leroy was bringing **cheese puffs**, **D**erek had jelly snakes and **N**orman wasn't sure what he was bringing. He was going to decide on the day.

One of my favourite things about going to the CINEMA is getting a box of **Chocteezers** as a treat. ☺

I'd promised my friends that I'd SHARE them.

(Not the WHOLE box – they'd understand.)

Derek was so ~~quick~~ quick to come round that I wasn't ready, and Delia got to the door before me.

IT'S THE **SWAMP MONSTER** ARGHH... Oh.

Hello, Delia. It was a joke for Tom,

Derek said, still swinging jelly snakes from his head. "Really? I'd never have guessed," Delia told him with a straight face.

"The snakes suit you," Delia said.

I came to his rescue just in time.

"YES! JELLY SNAKES! Can I have one now?"

Derek passed one over.

"That's been in Derek's hair, Tom!"
Delia told me like that was a problem.

"They weren't **IN** my hair, I was just
holding them near it," Derek said.
He offered Delia a snake as well.
"Want one?"

Ewwwww.

It was nice of him, but Delia wasn't keen.

I ate my snake like it was a piece of spaghetti,
holding it above my mouth and dropping it down.

(The first of many treats that day ... mmmm.)

Dad was in the kitchen and asked what film we were going to see.

SWAMP MONSTER 3.

we told him in our best **MONSTER** voices.

"I might come and see it with you. That sounds like FUN!" Dad said.

NO! You can't! I answered a bit too fast.

We'd planned to go to the **CINEMA CLUB** with just our friends (and snacks), not with Dad.

"You could give us a lift though, so we're not late?" I added.

Dad **LAUGHED.** "I suppose I could."

"And maybe buy us some drinks and a box of **Chocteezers?**"

I thought it was worth asking.

Derek gave him a jelly snake so he didn't feel bad.

Dad ate the jelly snake and took us to the CInema EARLY so we could get the GOOD seats.

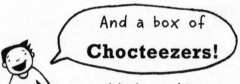

The kids' club is ALWAYS popular and **SWAMP MONSTER 3** was a film LOADS of kids wanted to see.

It was already packed when we arrived.

Dad signed us in, and we put on our wristbands.

"You two go and join the queue and I'll get some drinks for you," Dad told us.

And a box of **Chocteezers!**

I added quickly in case he'd forgotten.

"YOU'LL NEVER GUESS WHO'S AT THE FRONT OF THE QUEUE!"

Derek said, sounding excited.

"Not Marcus...?" I sighed.

It was ONLY LEROY AND Norman!

They were standing right next to the cinema

entrance, which was ☆IMPRESSIVE. We'd all be first

inside now!

We ran over to join them and let the other kids

in the queue know we <u>WEREN'T</u> pushing in. (No one

likes a pusher in.)

"Nice work, guys, now we can all get seats

together," I said happily.

We compared snacks while waiting

for Dad and worked out how to

divide them up.

Norman had brought toast in a

lunch box. (Random.)

"It's got chocolate spread on it, cut into fingers

so we can share it," he said, which made sense.

Then I heard one of my FAVOURITE sounds EVER...

rattle

rattle

rattle

rattle

A FULL BOX OF CHOCTEEZERS.

Yes!

I could tell Norman was rethinking his toast.

"Don't panic... I'll share them," I assured him.

(Not the WHOLE box, obviously.)

Dad passed me the **Chocteezers** and gave
Norman and Leroy their drinks.

"Are you staying for the film, Mr Gates?"
Leroy asked.

"I could do," Dad said, surprising me. "But I won't.
Enjoy the film. Behave, Tom, and I'll meet you all
here after."

"And don't forget ...

I'LL BE BACK!"

(He said this in a very deep, very loud voice.)

"Thanks, Dad," I said and waved him goodbye

(before he did THAT voice again).

"Does your dad always talk like that?" asked Leroy.

"Only in front of my friends."

I noticed Leroy had brought a LARGE

bag with him – that looked promising.

"I've got **cheese puffs.** One bag for each of

us," he said. "And a cushion in case someone

tall sits in front of me."

(Leroy had thought of everything.)

"We should PLAN where we're going to sit

before we go in," Derek suggested.

"We can sit ANYWHERE we want to –

we're FIRST in the QUEUE!"

Norman reminded us.

We had a BIG chat about all the BEST places to sit. Norman likes being in the middle, Derek at the back, Leroy thought four seats at the side would be good, and I like sitting at the front. We were so busy talking that we didn't notice the queue had started to move ...

IN THE OTHER DIRECTION.

No!

This was a DISASTER.

We'd been standing at the WRONG DOOR and now we were right at the BACK and all the good seats would be gone!

"Come on! Let's just go to the front," Derek suggested.

But when we got there, the kids' club lady told us to wait in line.

"There's no hurry, you'll all get in.

It's a $\mathbb{BIG}$ CINEMA," she said.

Yeah, NO pushing in! someone in the queue shouted.
(Marcus Meldrew.)

"We were here FIRST - at the wrong door!"
I tried to explain.

But it was no good. We had to go all the way to the BACK, walking past AMY, Florence and Marcus, who waved.

"You should have got here earlier."
He smiled.

It was very annoying. Derek was FUMING, so to lighten the mood I opened the **Chocteezers** and offered them round (which helped).

At least the queue moved pretty fast and it didn't take long to get to the front, where we showed our wristbands and went inside. Only to find all the good seats were GONE. The whole cinema was FULL and trying to find FOUR seats all together was looking impossible. 😥

"Are we going to have to sit separately and not share our snacks?" Leroy asked.

"No! Let's keep looking," I said.

Then Norman shouted,

"OVER THERE!" ------>

and pointed to FOUR SEATS one row back from the front. We ran as fast as we could and grabbed them before anyone sat there.

I even had two spare seats next to me.

Things were looking UP. ☺

Until the TALLEST grown-up sat in front of Leroy.

He just reached into his bag, got out the cushion,

and was instantly LIFTED UP (like magic!).

(Cushions rule...) Leroy said.

(I had cushion envy as Leroy looked EXTRA

comfy too.)

Before the film started, we got settled and shared

out the snacks. I passed my **Chocteezers** down

so everyone could take some and I tried not to

JUDGE when Norman took quite a lot.

Then I carefully put my box on the EMPTY

Huh?

SEAT next to me. Waiting for the film to

start, I had a few cheese puffs before the adverts

finished and the lights went down ...

... when two latecomers sat in the empty seats next to me RIGHT ON MY **Chocteezers**.

I had a moment of PANIC before I spotted them on the arm rest between the seats. It was a HUGE relief, until I heard the NOISE of my **Chocteezers** moving around.

Someone was TAKING them!

This was a VERY **BAD** situation that I needed to
STOP right away. I reached down to take MY
Chocteezers back, but the kid next to
me was already holding them. They took my
Chocteezers and ...

OPENED them!

I was just about to SHOUT OUT:

"HEY! Those are MINE!"

when I heard the kid say:

Chocteezers are the BEST.

I FROZE. I recognized that voice. Of ALL the
kids to sit next to me, why did it have to be

BUSTER JONES?

He was always getting in trouble at school.

WHAT was I going to do? Most of the time it was best to AVOID Buster or you'd end up in detention.

Avoiding him now was going to be IMPOSSIBLE! I whispered to Derek, "Buster Jones is sitting next to me, and he's taken my Chocteezers."

Derek gulped, leaned forwards, then back.

"Don't make eye contact. He doesn't know it's you," Derek told me, and passed the message on to Leroy and Norman, who also took a sneaky peek. Norman passed me some of his chocolate-spread toast.

"Norman says you should eat this instead – to avoid any trouble," Derek said.
It was good advice.

No one liked standing up to **Buster Jones.**

But these were <u>MY</u> **Chocteezers,** and it wasn't FAIR.

I took a deep breath ... and slowly, quietly, began to put my hand into the box.

The **Chocteezers** kept rolling around and were very noisy. But I managed to eat a handful without **Buster** noticing.

(I'd just <u>SHOW</u> him they were mine.)

Buster picked the box up and passed it to his friend.

"**Help yourself,**" I heard him say...

(Oh no...)

THIS IS A DISASTER!

Buster's friend was eating them now. I didn't want to get on the WRONG side of **Buster** (or his friend). I tried to concentrate on the film, but all I could hear were my **Chocteezers** being eaten ...

... and not by <u>me</u>.

I just had to sit quietly until **Buster** put <u>my</u> box back on the armrest. I took my chance and tried to eat some more before they were all gone. The box was nearly ⚡EMPTY⚡. I had to be BRAVE and pluck up the courage to tell **Buster** to stop eating my **Chocteezers!**

I decided to wait for the right time to say
something.

I waited ...

and waited ...

(ate some toast)

and then waited some more.

Just as the film finished and the credits began to
roll, I took a deep breath.

Derek nudged me.

"Good film, wasn't it?" he asked.

"I wouldn't know. It was hard to FOCUS,"
I whispered, pointing in **Buster's** direction.
"I'm going to tell him they were mine," I added.

"That's going to be hard," Derek said.

"I know but I HAVE to say something..."

"**No,** you can't..."

"Why Not?"

"Because he's already gone!" Derek said.

I turned around and sure enough, **Buster** and his friend had left, leaving behind my VERY empty **Chocteezers** box. I'd missed out on EVERYTHING: the film AND my treats.

I picked up the empty box and showed it to Norman, Leroy and Derek.

"Sorry about the **Chocteezers**, Tom. Here, have the last piece of chocolate-spread toast," Norman said, but the toast looked a bit squashed so I didn't take it.

Dad would be waiting outside, so we began to make our way past the other seats when my foot touched something on the floor.

I bent down to take a look only to find...

The box that **Buster** <u>must</u> have moved when he sat down. I suddenly realized I'd been helping myself to **Buster Jones's Chocteezers** the WHOLE TIME.  Sneaking handfuls whenever I could.

I shuddered and tried not to think about what **Buster Jones** would have done if he'd caught me.

GATESY, you ate my Chocteezers!

I was just very happy to find my treats.

And I wasn't the only one...

Leroy, Derek and Norman were
SUPER happy I'd found another box!
The sound of them rattling wasn't as
loud as Dad's monster voice calling out:

"HOW WAS SWAMP MONSTER 3? DID YOU ENJOY THE FILM?"

"It was AMAZING, Mr Gates ...
especially the SONGS!" Leroy told him.

 "I missed the songs," I whispered.

"I can't believe you've still got a WHOLE box of
Chocteezers, Tom. It must have been a really
good film if you forgot to eat those!"

Dad LAUGHED.

"I might have to watch it again," I told him.

In the car going home, I shared the **Chocteezers** out.

By the time we'd dropped off

N orman ...

Bye! See you at school!

L eroy ...

See you! Thanks!

and D erek ...

BYE, Tom!

the **Chocteezers** were (nearly) all gone.

I managed to eat the last few before Delia saw them.

And the lovely smell of chocolate has STAYED in the box for a very long time.

Every now and then I like to pick up the box and remember when it was filled with **Chocteezers** in the cinema, while trying hard to forget about **Buster Jones.**

Mmmm mmm

(I still haven't seen SWAMP MONSTER 3, though!)

I spent a bit of time doodling on the empty box
lid with my special pen.

It looks even nicer now.

If I got ★ ★ ★ ★ ★ for this story, I would celebrate with some **Chocteezers**

(obviously).

best treat
↓

I **STILL** can't decide what I should write about to get into the FIRST EVER Oakfield School book of FUNNY STORIES.

Even the pen I'm holding has a FUNNY STORY behind it. Granny Mavis bought it for me. It's the BEST pen in the WHOLE WIDE **WORLD**.

(Really!)

It writes on most things like paper, wood, shoes, my pencil case, stones and other things too. — Dad's hat

Here's the story of how I got my special pen...

GET PERMISSION!

WARNING!
Don't draw on stuff you're not allowed to.

When I am very old (like **THE FOSSILS**), I will STILL be using my special pen to draw on things (hopefully). ☺

old Tom

My special pen.

I drew on this case when I was very young!

I'm trying **hard** not to lose it because I can be a bit forgetful.

One trick I have is to TIE a piece of string to my pen. When Marcus Meldrew TOOK it, he got a bit of a **SURPRISE**. I pulled the string and pinged the pen right back into my hands. ⊙ ⊙

That's MY pen, Marcus, thank you.

Hey! I was using that!

This may seem a bit EXTREME, but it does stop stuff from going missing.

Mum likes to pretend she NEVER loses things, but I know she does.

Once she bought a book about how to be organized and tidy.

"This book is going to CHANGE OUR LIVES. We all need to be more tidy in this house."

Then she put the book down somewhere and lost it. Mum looked everywhere. Eventually, I was the one who found it under a big pile of magazines. →

"I think you need this book more than I do..." I said.

"I wondered where that went!"

Dad loved telling ANYONE who'd listen how Mum had lost the tidy book.

She bought a book on tidying and lost it!

Ha! Ha!

Dad loses things too.

Once I saw him on his phone talking to Mum.

Rita, do you know where my phone is?

I can't find it.

All the time it was in his hand...

Mum likes telling THAT story.

Can you believe it was in his hand?

Ha! Ha!

Delia loses things as well...

She likes to blame ME when her sunglasses go missing.
(I admit sometimes I borrow them, **but** not always.)
Like the time they were on her head.

Tom, have you taken my sunglasses again?

"Errr, no, Delia."

Are you SURE?

Tom, come on. Go and get my glasses...

"No, I can't."

WHY NOT?

"Because they're on your head," I told her.

Ha! Ha! Ha!

Granny Mavis is VERY organized and doesn't often
lose things.

(She always knows where Granddad

has left his teeth.)

Here!

Once Granny came to see us on her roller skates.

She was on the way to buy some new glasses and

wondered if I wanted to come with her.

Wheeeee!

"I need to get some NEW frames and I
can't see what they look like. Could you
help me, Tom?" she asked.

Of course I said YES!

Granny Mavis is <u>ALWAYS</u> fun to hang out with.

"It will be lovely to have your company, Tom,"
Granny told me.

I took my mini scooter to try and keep up
with Granny on her skates.
(She has a LOT of energy.)

We got to the opticians in no time at all.
It was easy to see the sign outside that said:

GREAT exSPECStations.

Granny took off her skates and I left my scooter in
a safe place by the door.
Then I followed her into the HUGE shop to help
choose some fancy new glasses.

Inside I'd never seen SO MANY pairs of glasses. There were FRAMES of all different shapes and sizes. Rows and rows and rows of them.

"Right, Tom, let's get started. I need you to say if they suit me. I can't see a thing without my REAL glasses," Granny explained.

"OK, Granny," I said, then I tried her glasses on for fun. Everything looked BLURRY so I took them off.

Granny was already wearing a pair of BIG round frames.

"How about these, Tom?" she asked.

"They make you look like a rockstar, Granny."

"Excellent, let's keep them." She LAUGHED.

Love them!

Granny spent a really long time trying on EVERY
kind of shape of glasses you could imagine. Square
shaped, star glasses, oval, wobbly frames, until finally ...

... she found a pair she liked.
"I like these, Tom. Let's get them. Now where did
you put my REAL glasses?" Granny asked me.
It was a VERY good question as neither of us
could see them. (Especially Granny.)
    "They're here somewhere," I muttered.

"Oh no, Tom, you haven't?" Granny said.

(I had...)

They could be ANYWHERE in the shop.

We walked UP and DOWN, tracing our steps back and looking on EVERY shelf. "It's not good, Tom.

Oh...

Nope, not these.

This is going to take forever." Granny sighed. Then I spotted a lady trying on what looked like Granny's glasses and admiring her reflection in a mirror.

"These lovely OLD vintage glasses are JUST what I've been looking for. They're PERFECT. I'll take them!" she said.

"I think I found them, Granny!" I said and rushed over to explain that the glasses weren't for sale. "I'm sorry. Those belong to my granny. She's over there waving at you," I told the lady, who was very nice and waved back. "She can't see you because you're wearing her glasses," I pointed out.

Granny was super grateful, and we had a good LAUGH about her glasses once she got them back.

"Now I know how your granddad feels when he loses his teeth," she told me.

(That's happened a few times before.) ☺

Once Granny had ordered her new glasses, we decided to walk back to her house. Granny said she'd had enough excitement for one day.

"I've got another `job` for you, Tom," she told me.

Oh... OK, I said. BUT, even though I like helping THE FOSSILS, the word JOB made me think it wouldn't be much fun.

So when we got back to the house and Granny gave me the special PEN,

I was EXCITED.

WOW! Thanks, Granny!

"You can decorate the ends of my glasses so I'll always be able to SPOT them in the shop," she told me.

(DREAM JOB!)

I decorated the ends of Granny's glasses with my EXPERT doodles.

And her glasses case too.

GRANNY'S glasses in here.

"Now, Tom ...

even though this pen draws on

loads of different things, always

ask permission before you draw on anything. You

don't want to get into trouble,"

Granny reminded me.

"Yes, Granny."

I did TRY and remember that ...

... most of the time.

(The stars came

off eventually...)

Delia doesn't love my special pen as much as I do. When I was younger, She used to tell me stories.

Then I'd tell THOSE stories to my friends and discover THEY WEREN'T TRUE.

"Did Delia tell you that?" Derek would say. Now I'm older, I'm not fooled by her NONSENSE.

Here are Delia's top four made-up stories:

- Eating the crusts on your
  bread will make your hair curly.

- If you eat FRUIT with pips, the
  pips will grow in your tummy
  and out of your ears.

- Delia said she had special powers
  and could talk to animals.

- Cabbage makes you taller.

 (Delia's nonsense.)

After a **long** time staring at all my stuff and thinking about the stories that go with them: *Great-Aunt Aggie's Hat*, my stone with a hole, the empty **Chocteezers** box, my special pen, I know what I'm going to write about.

I can't get distracted by ANYTHING or I'll be late handing it in, and then I won't get

FIVE STARS.

Here goes...

funny story-concentrating face

(Just doing my five-star doodle first.)

Five-star distraction bugs.

I finished my story and handed it in ON TIME
(result!).

AMY asks me what I wrote about.

"Something FUNNY, I hope!" I tell her.

"I wrote a FUNNY poem," AMY says.

"Isn't it supposed to be a STORY?" Marcus joins in.

"Mr Fullerman said a poem's OK too.
It's a FUNNY poem, so I hope it gets into
the book. It's about socks," AMY tells us.

"My story is VERY FUNNY. I wrote about something
that happened to me,"

Marcus says very confidently.

"So did I," I say.

I wonder what stories will make it into Oakfield School's first ever

FIVE-STAR STORY BOOK.

(Not long to wait.)

random bat

Hey, look at that bat up there!

Oh yeah! A bat!

Not looking because I know you're making it up!

"Well done, **EVERYONE!**
You should be very proud of
yourselves. <u>**AND**</u> even if you're
not in **<u>THIS</u>** book, you'll get a
special certificate, a badge and a
smiley face sticker,"
Mr Fullerman said.

(He's in a VERY good mood.)

"I enjoyed reading **ALL** your poems and stories. I've learnt about what makes you laugh and I had a lot of **LAUGHS** myself. It won't be long before you'll be **able to read** Oakfield School's first **EVER** book of **FIVE-STAR STORIES.**"

Sir! Sir! Did you like my cheese and dragons story?

"I liked all the stories, Norman."

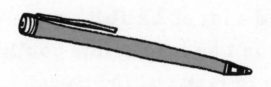

Finally! Here's my copy.

I put a sticker
on it so everyone knows
it's mine.

Oakfield School Five-Star Stories

Volume 1

★ ★ ★ ★ ★

Stories, poems and
other funny stuff by
the pupils of
Oakfield School

Tom Gates

This book belongs to:

Tom Gates
(because I got 5 stars!)

Welcome to the first ever
FUNNY FIVE-STAR STORIES book.

Congratulations to everyone who took part.

If you got five stars for your work, WELL DONE!

We hope it encourages you to keep on

writing your funny stories and poems

so we can make another book.

Oakfield School
Five-Star Stories

★ ★ ★ ★ ★

By the pupils of
Oakfield School

I added
a bug!

Published by
Oakfield School

Here's Florence Mitchell trying not to laugh while singing **"The Silly Song of Sounds"** with her band **Florence and the Smiley Faces.**

The Silly Song of Sounds
By Florence Mitchell

(Absolutely NO LAUGHING when you say this.)

Yippy Yappy

Yeah Yeah

Yippy Yappy Yoooo

Fribble Frabble FROO FROO

Wibble Wobble Woo

Hippy Happy HAY HEY

Yippy Yappy YOU!

HIPPY HOPPY

Hoo Hoo

Hippy Happy

Hey!

(Repeat as many times as you can.)

FUN AND NAMES

BY* ...

(This story didn't have a name on it but is being included because **Mr Keen** has a good idea who it might be and we all enjoyed it.)

Mr Tedious was the head teacher of Snoore School, the most **BORING** school in the whole wide world. *EVERYTHING* about the school was **DULL.**

← yawn

The lessons were MIND-NUMBINGLY boring.

yawn

Mr Tedious had the dreariest (voice) EVER. It sent all the children to sleep.

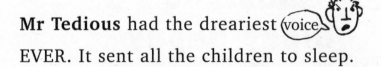

*Mystery kid who wrote this story.

This was a **HUGE** problem because **Mr Tedious** was also *MEAN* and anyone who didn't stay awake would get a

BIG BORING DETENTION.

The children tried **VERY** hard to pay attention and keep their eyes open.
__But__ it wasn't easy.

Every morning the day would start like this...

Mr Tedious would stand in front of the **WHOLE school** and read out a list of children who'd  ᶻᶻᶻᶻᶻᶻᶻᶻᶻ *FALLEN ASLEEP* in lessons.

It was a

VERY

LONG

LIST

and by the time he'd finished reading it, even **MORE** children were *asleep.*
(Sooo boring.)

 ᶻᶻᶻᶻᶻᶻᶻᶻᶻ

Mr Tedious would *shout,*

"You there! Stop snoozing! Wake up! You are in detention!"

(This happened EVERY DAY.)

What?

No, sir!

I'm awake!

Lessons were a snoozefest too. Then one day after a particularly **BORING** lesson, one kid (a hero ⟶ who can't be named for a good reason) said to the other kids that **SOMETHING** had to change.

I have a plan.

"**Mr Tedious** is SO **DULL** it's impossible to stay **AWAKE** listening to him!" EVERYONE agreed.

It's true. It's not our fault we can't stay awake. The list is SO BORING!

the other kids said.

"I'm going to **ADD** some **EXTRA** names to the list that will **CHEER** us up, make us *laugh* and keep us **awake!**" the kid (who can't be named) told them.

"**How are you going to do that?**" the other kids asked.

"I will be **EXTRA** careful, don't worry. **I'm SMART.**"

The **next** morning, the kid (who can't be named) *snuck* into the school office and CAREFULLY added some **EXTRA** names to **Mr Tedious's** list.

(The kid tried not to *laugh* **too much** as the names were making **them giggle.)**

The kid (who can't be named) was really looking forward to school assembly now.

Ha! Ha! Ha! Ha!

The next day, as he was reading the list, **Mr Tedious** narrowed his eyes and **STARED** at anyone who was making a noise.

Keep quiet or you'll be in detention tomorrow!

he said, then carried on reading.

The kid (who can't be named) was enjoying this list. **Mr Tedious** cleared his throat.

Annette Curtain...

Annette Curtain.

This name also made the children laugh.

He *he* he *he* he *he* he *he* he!

You over there! Pull yourself together!

Mr Tedious snapped, which only made everyone laugh even more.

Mr Tedious fixed the children with a **stern, BORING** look.

Do you ALL want a detention?

This is NO LAUGHING MATTER.

No one wanted a detention, but this was funny!
The kid (who can't be named) was trying not
to **laugh.**

Mr Tedious waited for silence, then began
to read again.

Ben Deelegs...

**ELLI FANT,
Dan Druff.**

He! he! he! he! he! he! he!

**Sid Downer,
Anita Bath.**

Ha! ha! ha! ha! ha!

Phil Itupp.

He! he! he! he! he! he! he!

**Tim Burr,
Justin Case.**

By the time **Mr Tedious** got to the last name on the list ...

... the children thought they would **EXPLODE** into a fit of **giggles** from trying to keep it all inside, including **the kid** (who can't be named).

They were **all** doing **so well** right up until **Mr Tedious** said the **last** child in detention was...

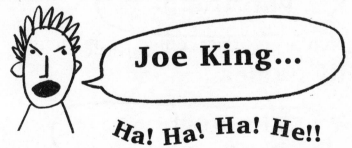

Joe King...

Ha! Ha! Ha! He!!

The **whole** school **burst** out *laughing* and couldn't stop for a very long time.

Mr Tedious wasn't happy.

 **"NO LAUGHING!**

What **do you** think school is **FOR?**

You're **NOT HERE** to **ENJOY YOURSELVES!"**

he told them.

"You're ALL in
DETENTION!"

The kids didn't care; they couldn't stop laughing at the **silly names**.

Mr Tedious wasn't used to the sound of children having **FUN** and began to *SLOWLY* dissolve into a **BIG** puddle of *DULLNESS.* No one had to have a **BORING** detention **EVER** again.

The boy (who can't be named) was a hero.

The end.

A poem about my missing sock

By Amy Porter

Where are you, sock?

Where have you gone?

I keep wishing

That you weren't missing

So I could wear

You as a pair.

Can you find the
pairs of socks?

The VERY Annoying Boys and the **Super Smart Kid**

By Marcus Meldrew

Once upon a time, there were two VERY annoying boys who liked to play silly games **ALL** the time.

They enjoyed making people **LOOK** at things that weren't really there.

It was a **RIDICULOUS** game. The boys thought they were SOOOOO clever, but let **ME** tell you – **THEY WERE NOT.**

One day, the boys decided to POINT at the sky and say...

"LOOK, EVERYONE, THERE'S A SPACESHIP! DID YOU SEE IT?"

The other children STARED at the sky and believed them, apart from one **smart** kid* who wasn't falling for their **NONSENSE.**

"You haven't seen anything. You're making it up!" the **smart** kid told them.

"We did see something!" the two **annoying** boys said and laughed at ALL the children they had made STARE at nothing.

"If you keep doing that, no one will ever believe you when you DO see something like a **spaceship**."

* Me

The two **annoying** boys didn't care.

"Whatever," they scoffed.

Then one day the **smart** kid looked up at the sky and really **DID** see a **spaceship!**

"Look up at the sky!" he said to the **annoying** boys. "There actually is a **spaceship** this time!"

But the two annoying boys were **TWITS** and **didn't** listen to him.

"Hey! That's OUR game. We're not falling for that," they said.

Twits. →

They IGNORED the **spaceship** that was now **HOVERING OVER THEIR HEADS**

(for real).

The **smart** kid watched the spaceship open its door.

"You should look up, it's amazing!" he said, trying to make them take notice.

"Blah, blah, blah... We know there's nothing there," the boys said.

Then a *L O N G* green
ALIEN arm came down,
scooped them
both up
and took
them away.

"Oh well, I did TRY and warn them," the **smart** kid said and waved them **goodbye.**

He had a nice *peaceful* afternoon until the **ALIENS** dropped the two annoying boys back down to earth, because even the **ALIENS** found them

ANNOYING.

THE END.

(And the **smart** boy lived happily ever after.)

This is not a story, but a collection of WORDS.

FUNNY WORDS that Make Me Laugh

By Julia Morton

Ha! Ha! Ha! Ha! Ha! Ha!

Kerfuffle

A disturbance or a bit of a fuss going on.

Ha!

DOLLOP

Shapeless blob of something — like cream.

Wobble

To move unsteadily (or when you're angry or upset).

Ha!

NITWIT

A silly or foolish person.

Ha! Ha!

Gobbledygook

Language that is meaningless and not easy to understand.

Ha!

Bumfuzzle

When you're a bit confused or bewildered (or both).

Ha! Ha! Ha!

The Dragon and the Cheese

By Norman Watson

Once upon a time, there was a town that made the BIGGEST and most delicious cheese in the whole wide world.

Everyone who lived in the town LOVED cheese. They even had a special

CHEESE PARTY DAY.

People would come from FAR and WIDE to taste the cheese at the party. This year there was GREAT excitement as the CHEESE looked even more delicious.

delicious cheese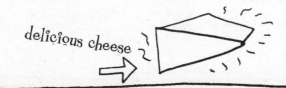

But the smell of the cheese had attracted
attention from a

DRAGON

who decided to FLY into the town and join in
the FUN at the party. The dragon had never
tasted cheese before.

"It's good to try new things," the dragon said.

The people of the town didn't agree.

They saw the DRAGON looming

towards their GIANT CHEESE

and shouted,

"BACK AWAY FROM

THE GIANT CHEESE. IT'S OURS!"

The dragon didn't like being told what to do

and got the HUMP. It had a bad temper

and began to ...

... HUFF and PUFF fire EVERYWHERE!

The **DRAGON** spoilt the whole cheese party and the townsfolk had to run for cover.

When the fire brigade came to put out the fire, the dragon HUFFED some more and turned all the water into STEAM. The townsfolk didn't know what to do. Then a smart girl stepped forward with an excellent plan.

"We need a HUGE loaf of bread and lots of CRACKERS," she told everyone. They thought she had lost the 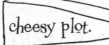 cheesy plot.

"Trust me, we WILL have a cheesy party and the DRAGON can help us."

(The dragon wasn't so sure.)

The smart girl went to talk to the dragon.

(She was brave as well as smart.)

"Listen up, dragon, we'll let you have some cheese, but you have to be helpful," she said.

The dragon was very hungry and reluctantly decided

to help.

Then the little girl asked all the townsfolk
to line up their loaves of bread next to the

GIANT CHEESE.

The dragon took a deep breath in and out
and the FLAMES that shot out of its mouth
toasted the bread and melted the cheese so it
bubbled and crisped up, looking even more
delicious!

The townsfolk began to tuck in to the toasted
bread and melted cheese

and dipped their crackers in too.

 The little girl gave some to the dragon, who thought it was DELICIOUS!

Everyone was happy. The girl had found a way to make the cheese party a big success <u>WITH</u> the dragon.

From then on, the townsfolk <u>ALWAYS</u> invited the dragon to the cheese party to toast the bread, melt the cheese and join in with the dancing.

When the little girl wanted to take a photograph, can you guess what the dragon said...?

THE END.

The MAGIC trick
By Leroy Lewis

I'm going to **SHARE** with you the *secret* of

how I can make things disappear. This magic trick

has been passed down from one magician

to another over many **hundreds** of years.

Every magician learns this trick and is careful

NEVER to give away the secret of how it's done.

So can YOU keep a secret?

GOOD! Because you are about to be **AMAZED**.

Say these magic words after me and wave your

hands around at the same time...

Abracadabra – cadabra – BOO!

Now turn the page...

(It worked... See! Nothing there!)

I am a magician after all.

YES!

My story about *Great-Aunt Aggie's hat*

got **FIVE STARS** from
Mr Fullerman and made

it into the book!

This certificate
is presented to
TOM GATES

for taking part in
the five-star story
project.

☆ ☆ ☆ ☆ ☆

Congratulations
from Oakfield School.

Mr Fullerman gave the WHOLE CLASS a certificate, a badge and a sticker for taking part in the FIVE-STAR STORY project even if your story didn't get in the book.

How brilliant is that?

(VERY.)

Derek's story about Rooster rolling in mud didn't get five stars, but he did get a SMILEY FACE ☺ on the <u>class</u> chart for being helpful.

⬆

That put him at the TOP of the chart, making him ★ star pupil for the week.

His mum and dad gave him a little extra pocket money for doing so well. Derek told me he got a special pen (like mine) and a box of **Chocteezers**, which he's going to share. ☺

(More good news!)

← special pen

rattle
rattle

To celebrate the new book, we had a special assembly and some kids (not me) read out their stories and poems.

Buster Jones didn't want to read his story about **Mr Tedious** out. He pretended it wasn't his story. (It was.)

I didn't write it. It's not mine.

M̶r K̶een said that <u>HE</u> would read the story instead, and when the

started LAUGHING at the silly names, **Buster** looked surprised.

"Maybe I did write it after all," he admitted and enjoyed the round of applause at the end.

(I'm still not telling him I ate his **Chocteezers** though ... no need.)

When Mum and Dad saw the book,
they LOVED it and didn't seem to mind
I'd ordered EXTRA copies to give out
to the family.

 △—Proud
face

Delia said she didn't need one.

"No, thanks. What I'm hoping for is another
decorated stone, Tom," she told me.

"Really?" I asked.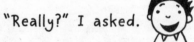

"No, I'm joking. And you'd better not have
written a story about ME," she added.

"No, not this time. I wrote about Granddad's
Great-Aunt Aggie's hat."

Mum and Dad looked surprised
like they didn't know.

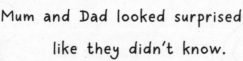

(218)

"It's a **FUNNY STORY**, especially the bit about the CAT jumping on top of the hat and messing it all up so you had to FIX it, Mum!" I reminded them.

"Oh, yes. You've written it all down here, haven't you, Tom?" Mum said as she read the story.

"I have!"

"Maybe we shouldn't give a copy to Granddad yet. He still doesn't know <u>exactly</u> what happened to the hat," Mum told me

(a bit too late).

Oh.

(Luckily **THE FOSSILS** were very impressed
with Mum's "fixing" skills and they
enjoyed my story.) ☺

Thanks to the book, there's a new CRAZE going around school where EVERYONE is trying to say Florence's song lyrics really fast without LAUGHING or making a mistake.

I'm not sure Mr Fullerman is enjoying the craze as much as we are.

Although I'm still playing the old game that Derek and I made up...

(Still looking...)

Draw a step-by-step BIRD from
Great-Aunt Aggie's hat.

And here's an
aardvark!

MAKE A CLAY BUG

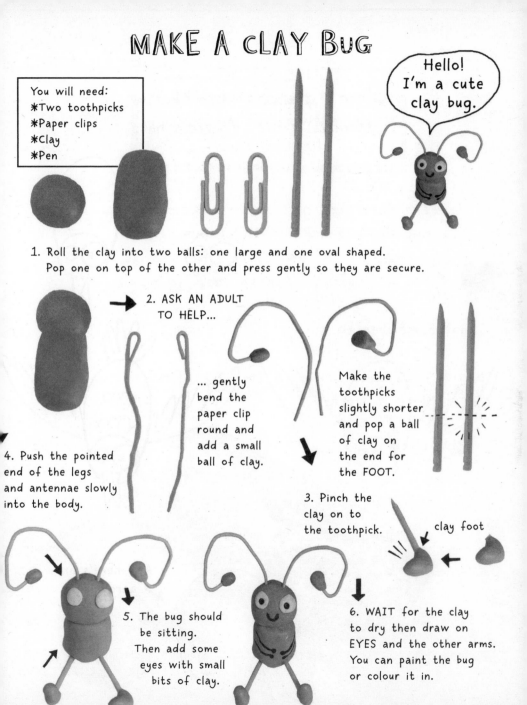

You will need:
* Two toothpicks
* Paper clips
* Clay
* Pen

Hello! I'm a cute clay bug.

1. Roll the clay into two balls: one large and one oval shaped. Pop one on top of the other and press gently so they are secure.

2. ASK AN ADULT TO HELP...

... gently bend the paper clip round and add a small ball of clay.

Make the toothpicks slightly shorter and pop a ball of clay on the end for the FOOT.

4. Push the pointed end of the legs and antennae slowly into the body.

3. Pinch the clay on to the toothpick.

clay foot

5. The bug should be sitting. Then add some eyes with small bits of clay.

6. WAIT for the clay to dry then draw on EYES and the other arms. You can paint the bug or colour it in.

More fun stuff at these websites:

thebrilliantworldoftomgates.com
lizpichon.com

Here's a decorated glasses case using a special pen.
You can also use a PERMANENT pen.
(Follow instructions on the pen as to what
surfaces it works on. Ask an adult to help.)

But remember to always:
* Get permission before drawing on anything.
* TEST your pen on a tiny area first to make
  sure it works.

GET BUSY doodling!

Answers to
the sock pairs.

Star bug answers: the star bugs can be found on
pages 40, 108, 127, 162 and 221.

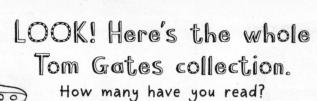

LOOK! Here's the whole Tom Gates collection.

How many have you read?

www.thebrilliantworldoftomgates.com

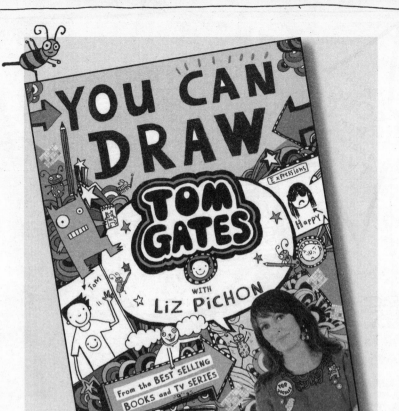

Learn to draw step-by-step people, places
and objects from Tom's world.

The must-have art activity

book for fans of

Tom Gates.

From **DOGZOMBIES** to **DUDE3**, music is a HUGE part of the Tom Gates world. Learn how to play all your favourite songs from the series with REAL notation for:

- Guitar
- Piano
- Ukulele
- Recorder

And with notation for drums and tips and tricks for vocals!

Read all the Tom Gates books?
Well now you can read *SHOE WARS*, a
standalone adventure story.

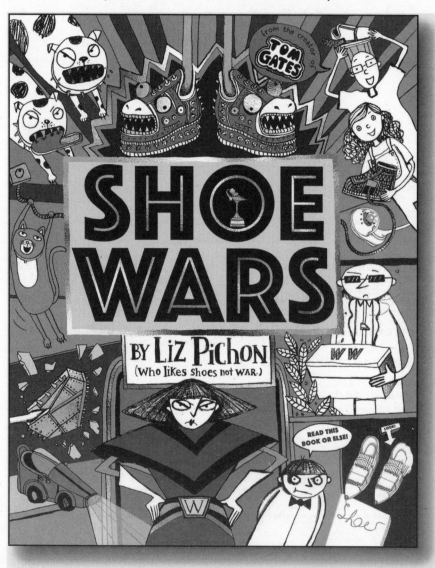

Welcome to Shoe Town – and meet Ruby and Bear Foot. They are running out of time to rescue their inventor dad from his hideous boss, Wendy Wedge. She'll do ANYTHING to win the glitzy Golden Shoe Award and knows that entering flying shoes is her hot ticket to the trophy. Flying shoes that Ruby and Bear just happen to be hiding...

Liz Pichon is one of the UK's best-loved and bestselling creators of children's books.

Her TOM GATES series has been translated into 45 languages, sold millions of copies worldwide, and has won the Roald Dahl Funny Prize, the Blue Peter Book Award for Best Story and the younger fiction category of the Waterstones Children's Book Prize.

In the eleven years since THE BRILLIANT WORLD OF TOM GATES first published, the books have inspired the nation's children to get creative, whether that's through reading, drawing, doodling, writing, making music or performing.

"I wanted to FILL the books with ALL the things I loved doing when I was a kid. It's just the best feeling ever to know children are enjoying reading the books, because I love making them. So thank you so much for choosing Tom Gates and keep reading and doodling!"

Visit Liz at www.lizpichon.com

(School photo of Liz being grum